# MY MOTHER'S HOUSE, MY FATHER'S HOUSE

The Seattle School of Theology & Psychology
2501 Elliott Ave.
Seattle, WA 98121
theseattleschool.edu

# MY MOTHER'S HOUSE, MY FATHER'S HOUSE

C.B. Christiansen

by C. B. Christiansen
illustrated by Irene Trivas

PUFFIN BOOKS

PUFFIN BOOKS
Published by the Penguin Group
Viking Penguin, a division of Penguin Books USA Inc.,
375 Hudson Street, New York, New York 10014, U.S.A.
Penguin Books Ltd, 27 Wrights Lane, London W8 5TZ, England
Penguin Books Australia Ltd, Ringwood, Victoria, Australia
Penguin Books Canada Ltd, 2801 John Street, Markham, Ontario, Canada L3R 1B4
Penguin Books (N.Z.) Ltd, 182–190 Wairau Road, Auckland 10, New Zealand

Penguin Books Ltd, Registered Offices: Harmondsworth, Middlesex, England

First published in the United States of America by Atheneum Publishers, 1989
Published in Picture Puffins 1990
1   3   5   7   9   10   8   6   4   2
Text copyright © C. B. Christiansen, 1989
Illustrations copyright © Irene Trivas, 1989
All rights reserved

LIBRARY OF CONGRESS CATALOGING IN PUBLICATION DATA
Christiansen, C. B.
My mother's house, my father's house / by C. B. Christiansen ;
illustrated by Irene Trivas.    p.   cm.
Summary: A child describes having two different houses in which to
live, "my mother's house" and "my father's house," and what it is
like to travel back and forth between them.
ISBN 0-14-054210-8
[1. Divorce—Fiction.   2. Parent and child—Fiction.]   I. Trivas,
Irene, ill.   II. Title.
PZ7.C45285My     1990     [E]—dc20      90-8289

Printed in Hong Kong
Set in Weiss

*To my suitcase friends,*
*especially Benjamin.*
*And to Roger.*
—C. B. C.


*To Lee Chapman*
— I. T.

My mother's house has seven rooms and one of
them is mine. I have a closet for my bat and ball
and skateboard and skis. I ride my bike to school.
My mother believes in exercise.

My father's house has three big rooms and
parts of each are mine. I have my own desk, a
drawer in the dresser, and a bed by the fireplace.
In the morning, my bed folds into a couch. My
father likes things neat.

When I grow up, I'll have a house with five
rooms, a fold-out couch, and a closet for my bat
and ball and skateboard and skis. I'll ride my bike
to work and pick up after myself.

My mother's house is filled with pictures. Her
camera clicks while we climb trees and visit the
zoo and plant our pumpkin seeds. My mother's
refrigerator is covered with snapshots and a finger
painting I made when I was four. Beside her bed,
in a silver frame, is a photograph of my mother
and me, together.

My father's house is filled with books. His
reading glasses bounce on his chest when we
walk to the park for a picnic. They rest on his
nose when we visit the library. Before he goes to
sleep, he puts them on his nightstand by the
ashtray I made when I was five. Beside the
ashtray is a leather scrapbook with photographs
of my father and me, together.

When I grow up, I'll have a house with books on the tables and pictures on the refrigerator. I'll visit the library and take picnics to the zoo. On my bedroom wall I'll hang a photograph of my mother and my father and me, together.

Before I go to my mother's house on Monday, Tuesday, Wednesday, and Thursday, my father tells me, "Don't forget to brush your teeth and say your prayers and mind your mother."

I pack my suitcase. He adds a roll of dental floss and my stuffed bear.

Before I go to my father's house on Friday,
Saturday, and Sunday, my mother tells me,
"Don't forget to do your homework and get some
fresh air and mind your father."

I pack my suitcase. She adds a pencil sharpener
and my tennis shoes.

When I grow up, I'll live in my house on

Monday . . .

Tuesday . . .

Wednesday . . .

Thursday . . .

Friday . . .

Saturday . . .

and Sunday. I'll have plenty of sharp
pencils and dental floss. But no suitcases.

My mother doesn't go into my father's house. She drops me off at the curb and I run up the steps. She waves from the car window. My father waves back. Our calico cat rubs against my leg and purrs hello. "Welcome home," my father says, as my mother drives away.

My father doesn't go into my mother's house.
He rides the bus with me to the corner where she
lives. I walk half a block to her driveway. Our
two black dogs lick my hand and bark hello.
"Welcome home," my mother says, as my father's
bus rumbles off.

When I grow up, I'll have a house that is
mine, all mine. I'll invite my father to share
my dresser and sleep on my fold-out couch.
I'll invite my mother to dig in my garden
and stay in my extra bedroom.

When I grow up, I'll have two black dogs and a calico cat and a mat on my doorstep that says *Welcome Home*.